Brittany's Big Surprise

by Deborah
Abrahamson

cover illustration by Chris Cocozza

To my husband Joe and our children:
Jen, Tim, Mike, and Becky for their love and encouragement;
to my many friends for their help and advice;
and a special thanks to "Grandma-Mom" Helen Hills
for the wonderful gift of imagination.
We all miss you.

Publishing Group ™

First printing by Willowisp Press 1998.

Published by PAGES Publishing Group
801 94th Avenue North, St. Petersburg, Florida 33702

Printed in the United States of America

Willowisp Press®

2 4 6 8 10 9 7 5 3 1

ISBN 0-87406-891-6

One

"WHE-E-E-E!" Molly squealed as I gave her another push on the swing. Her golden curls twirled around her sweet face. Molly's smile gave way to funny little baby giggles.

"Your sister is so-o-o cute," I said to my best friend, Charity McKay.

"Yeah, Brittany, she's real cute all right," Charity replied. "She was adorable when she toddled into my room around five o'clock this morning, too. The sun wasn't even up yet!"

I gave another push to the swing that dangled from one of the huge oak trees in the McKays' yard. Whenever I'm at Charity's house I feel as if I've gone somewhere way out in the country. That's because her house sits in the middle of a few acres. You can't even see any other houses nearby.

"Sometimes I daydream about what a

brother or sister of mine would have looked like," I said. "I never realized how different brothers and sisters could look from each other. I mean, look at you and Molly—you have straight, long, brown hair and brown eyes, but she has blond, curly hair and blue eyes. I look more like her than you do," I said, pointing to my own blond hair and blue eyes.

"You're right. Hey, I know," Charity said, smiling. "We'll invent a new game show, 'Guess The Family.' We'll be the first contestants." She put her hand up to her mouth as if she was holding onto an invisible microphone and spoke like a television announcer. "Okay, television audience, it's up to you to decide who is the sister of the mystery baby. Is it Contestant Number One . . .," she pointed to me as she spoke to our imaginary audience, ". . . or is it Number Two?" she added, pointing to herself. "Now let's get some clues from today's Mystery Baby." Charity put the pretend microphone up to Molly. "Okay, Mystery Baby, what clues do you have for our audience today?"

Molly spoke up in a loud voice, "Me fwing, me fwing."

"There you have it, audience, our first clue," Charity went on. "The baby likes to swing! Now let's see which of our fabulous contestants likes to swing. How about you, Contestant Number One? Do you like to swing?"

"I love to swing," I said, laughing.

"Contestant Number Two, do you like to swing?" Charity paused for a second before she spoke into the imaginary mike, and changed to a high-pitched voice, "Swinging makes me barf!"

I clutched my stomach and practically fell over laughing.

"Stop!" I pleaded. "You've gone completely crazy. I can't take much more!"

"Can you imagine if we included our parents in the game?" Charity asked. "No one would ever guess that I belonged with *my* parents. They both love organic gardening, health food, and recycling everything they possibly can. I hate working in the garden, love junk food, and love everything new."

"I'm not exactly like my parents either," I said. "I mean, I live in a new house, in a new neighborhood, but I think your old house is totally cool. I think it's so neat that you've lived here practically forever."

"I can't remember ever living anywhere else," Charity said. "After all, I was only two when we moved here ten years ago."

"You were the same age as Molly."

5

"Gosh, somehow I never thought of it that way before," Charity replied thoughtfully.

"I've lived in about six different houses in the same amount of time," I said. "That means that we've moved every other year." I looked over at the old wooden farmhouse— what they call a "cracker" house here in Florida. I especially loved the wide front porch with the tin roof that sounds like a drum when it rains. The inside of the house is different from mine, too. Charity thinks my house looks like the inside of a magazine. That's because my mother loves to decorate with everything new and color-coordinated, right down to the flowers on the tables.

"Your house is cozier than mine," I said. "You know how I love the antique furniture, the quilts and the old wicker baskets. It even smells different, like lemons and cinnamon and your mom's fresh-baked bread. I can't remember my mother ever baking much of anything, except maybe Christmas cookies."

"Your mom is too busy going to work," Charity answered. "Your parents are always taking clients out to dinner and stuff. My mom does her art work at home. It's different."

"That's for sure," I agreed. "My mother's been so busy working since we moved here two months ago that we hardly even have

6

dinner at home. And if that's not enough, lately she's been acting funny. She seems worn out and kind of grumpy."

"Geez, that's too bad," Charity replied. "What's wrong with her? I mean, is she sick?"

"I don't know," I said. "But the last time she acted like this, we were getting ready to move again. She is going to the doctor today. Maybe he can give her some medicine or something."

"That would be good. I mean the doctor part. I don't want you to move away," Charity said as she sighed loudly. "I'm getting tired of standing here. Let's go sit down on the porch."

"Good," I said, "because my arms feel like they're going to fall off from pushing this swing."

Charity lifted Molly out of the swing and carried her up to the porch with us. She put her down to play next to some of her toys. Charity's huge white Labrador lumbered over to little Molly and gave her a big kiss. Then he ran over to us and jumped up on the porch swing, right where we were planning to sit.

"Okay, Shakespeare," Charity said to the dog. "Get down. You know you're not allowed up there. You big, overgrown baby." He reluctantly got off the swing and laid down on the porch right beside Molly instead.

Before we even had a chance to sit down, Charity's seven-year-old brother Zachary shoved open the screen door and ran across the porch, practically knocking us over. He had an apron tied like a cape around his neck and his arms were stretched out in front of him as if he were flying. He yelled, "Superman to the rescue!"

"Will you knock it off, Zach?" Charity asked, annoyed.

"How do you expect me to save the world from the aliens?" he yelled in protest.

"There's no such thing as aliens, Zach," Charity replied.

"There are, too," he argued. "An alien spaceship crash-landed in Roswell, New Mexico, almost thirty years ago. They think a bunch of government scientists have kept the aliens hidden in some secret lab all these years. I read about it in my science fiction magazine."

Charity sighed and rolled her eyes. Her younger brother is not like most kids I know. He's super-smart. Because of that, he sometimes causes Charity some problems. He doesn't mean to—it's just that Zach's in his own little world most of the time—a world of encyclopedias, computers, gizmos, and gadgets. But sometimes, like when he's pretending to be Superman, he's just a normal little boy.

Charity shook her head at Zach as he ran down the steps and out into the yard. We finally sat down on the wooden porch swing.

"Be glad you don't have a brother like him," Charity commented.

"Aw, he's not so bad," I said.

"Not so bad? This morning there were ants crawling all over the hall upstairs. We didn't know it, but he had been collecting them in a jar. Zachary thought he would start his own ant farm. When he brought the jar upstairs, he dropped it on the floor. It makes my skin crawl every time I think about those ants all over the floor. Yuck!"

"Yeah, well, I can see where that was pretty gross," I agreed, "but he's not like that all the time. He can be sweet, too."

"Yeah, I guess," Charity replied reluctantly. "Besides, when it comes to my brother Zachary, there could never be enough room in the world for another one." We both laughed.

"Well, no matter what you say," I continued, "I'd still love to have a little brother or sister. It gets boring being an only child."

The sun was starting to go down. I could see Charity's mother through the kitchen window as she cooked dinner. It smelled wonderful.

"Well, it's starting to get dark and I have

to walk home, so I'd better get going," I said as I got up. "It's almost dinner time, already. Who knows? Maybe just once I'll be surprised with an actual home-cooked meal!"

*   *   *   *   *

When I got to my house and opened the door, I was amazed. I really did smell food cooking. My parents were making dinner together. I couldn't believe it.

"Wow!" I said. "A real dinner. My wish came true. What happened?"

My father was smiling and stirring away at the stove.

"We're celebrating," he replied cheerily.

"Celebrating what?" I asked.

"You'll see," my mother answered. "We'll tell you after dinner, dear."

"Oh, I hate it when you make me wait," I said, feeling annoyed. "Now I'll be wondering all through dinner what in the world you're celebrating. Please tell me you didn't get another job or something. I don't want to have to move again."

"Who said anything about a new job? It's nothing like that," my father said. "Anyway, dinner is ready, so you won't have to wait long. Come sit down."

"What are we having?" I asked.

"Chicken fajitas and salad," my mom replied.

"And," my father continued, "we stopped at the bakery and bought a chocolate cheese-cake for dessert."

"Yum!" I said. But I couldn't help imagining what they were both so happy about.

Finally, I couldn't stand the suspense any longer.

"So?" I said. "What's going on?"

"Well, I'm sure you've noticed that I haven't been feeling well for a while," my mother began.

I nodded. Now I was really confused. Why were they so happy if she wasn't feeling well?

"We were fairly convinced that we knew the reason," my mother continued, "but we didn't want to say anything to you until we knew for sure."

"And then we had to wait," my father chimed in, "until we knew that everything was okay."

"Yes," my mom agreed, "because we didn't want to disappoint you."

"Now wait a minute," I interrupted. "I don't understand any of this. What are you talking about? You're not making any sense."

"You see, dear," my father explained,

11

"your mother is expecting."

"Expecting what?" I asked.

"Why, Brittany," my mother replied patiently, "a baby, of course. We're expecting a baby."

My mouth dropped open. My smiling parents sat there looking at me. They reminded me of that Cheshire Cat in *Alice in Wonderland*. I was speechless for a minute.

I finally found some words.

"I can't believe it," I said. "I really can't."

"After twelve years, we couldn't believe it either," my dad replied.

Somehow it started to really sink in then. Me. Brittany Wilson. I was going to be a big sister!

I screamed and jumped up and down. I think I scared my parents.

"I think it's too much of a shock for her, dear," my father said to my mother.

I screamed again. Then I laughed.

"Oh my," I said. "Oh my, oh my, oh my," I stammered.

"Are you all right, Brittany?" my mother asked.

I nodded.

"So what do you think?" she questioned further.

"It's what I've always wanted," I said,

smiling. "I didn't think . . . I mean, I just assumed that you didn't want any more kids."

My mother replied, "We didn't think it was possible, Britt."

"Oh?" I was surprised to hear that. No one had ever told me that before.

"Your mother had lots of problems after you were born," my father explained. "We wanted more children, but, well, after a while we figured that it wasn't going to happen.

"But now, here we are," my mother said, smiling again, and looking all dreamy-eyed. "Who would have thought?"

I sat there, feeling as if someone just conked me on the head. The wheels in my brain were spinning about a million miles an hour.

"When?" I asked.

"You mean when is the baby due?" my mom asked. "In about four and a half months."

"Four and a half months!" I squealed. "I thought it usually took about nine months for these things to happen. How long have you known about this?"

"Well, honey," my mother explained, "because we didn't think it was possible . . . and then when we *did* suspect, we wanted to make sure that everything was okay."

"Is it?" I asked with concern. "Okay, I mean."

"Yes, honey, everything is fine," she replied. "I've had lots of tests. If we wanted to know, we could even find out if the baby is a boy or a girl."

"Oh, cool!" I said. "Do you know? Tell me. I want to know if I'm going to have a brother or a sister."

"Wait a minute, Britt," my mother went on. "I said . . . if we *wanted* to know. We decided that we wanted to wait to find out."

"That's right," my father agreed. "We told the doctor that we wanted to wait and have a happy surprise, just like the one we had on that wonderful day twelve years ago when you were born." He got up from the table and gave me a little hug.

"Oh, I can't wait to tell Charity," I said. "It's so weird. We were talking about brothers and sisters just today. I was telling her how lucky I thought she was. I can't wait to tell her. I'm going to go call her right now."

I jumped up from the table and ran upstairs to my room. I was so excited I could barely manage to press the buttons on my phone.

I heard it ring, and then Zach answered.

"Hello, this is the McKay residence. Please leave your message after the beep . . .

B-e-e-e-e-p."

"Zachary?"

No answer.

"Zachary, I know it's not an answering machine."

Still no answer.

"Zachary! Say hello."

"Hello."

"This is Brittany. May I speak to Charity?"

"Didn't you just leave here? Why do you want to talk to her already?" he asked.

"Zachary, it's important. Hurry up and go get her."

"What's so important?"

"ZACH!!!"

"All right already. I'll go get her."

It seemed like forever, but Charity finally picked up the phone.

"Hello?"

"Charity, it's me. Wait'll you hear what I have to tell you."

"What is it?"

"You're not going to believe it."

"What? Tell me already."

"You just won't believe it," I went on. "Well, you know what we were talking about this afternoon? How I always wished that I had a little brother or sister like you had?

Well, it looks like I'm going to get my wish."

"Do you mean what I think you mean?"

"Yep, I'm going to be a big sister. Can you believe it? My mom is going to have a baby."

"Oh, wow! That's so cool." Charity said. "I'm so happy for you."

"Just think," I added. "A cute little baby to play with. I can hold her, and play with her, and maybe I'll get to help feed her sometimes."

"You keep saying *her*," Charity interrupted. "The baby might be a *him*."

"Yeah, I know. I don't care if I have a little brother or sister. I'm just so happy."

"When is your brother or sister supposed to be born?"

"Mom said four and a half months."

"Wow! So soon? I thought you were going to say something like next spring. Does your mom look like she's getting fat?

"I haven't really noticed. She might look a little bigger. Hey, can you come over tomorrow? It's Saturday. We can talk some more."

"I have some chores, but I'll come over as soon as I can get done. Okay?"

"Okay, I'll see you tomorrow."

"Bye, big sister," Charity said.

"Oh, wow. Bye. See you tomorrow."

Two

ALL night long, I tossed and turned in my bed. I couldn't stop thinking about my future brother or sister. I even dreamed about the baby.

In my dream, there was a knock on my bedroom door. When I opened it, my parents were standing there. They were smiling. Then I noticed that my father was holding a bundle in his arms.

"Is the baby here already?" I asked.

My dad said, "Yes, Brittany, come see your new little brother."

But, when they opened the blanket to show me what the baby looked like, I had a tremendous shock! The baby didn't look the way a baby is supposed to look. It looked just like a miniature version of Zach!

As I was dreaming, I kept saying over and over, "Charity said there could never be room for another one!" I was so glad to wake up and find out that it was just a dream.

I got out of bed and went downstairs to eat breakfast. Then I went back up to my room and got dressed.

There was a lot of commotion outside. I looked out my bedroom window to see what it was. A moving van was parked next door, and some people were yelling directions as they began hauling boxes out of the back. It looked as if we were getting new neighbors.

I ran downstairs.

My mother was in the kitchen loading the breakfast dishes into the dishwasher.

"Oh, guess what, Brittany?" she said when she saw me.

"Not another surprise," I replied. "I don't think I could handle another one."

"Well, it's not exactly a surprise. We're going to have new neighbors."

"I saw the moving van already," I said.

"Well, I spoke to them this morning. They have a boy your age. In fact, he goes to your school."

This was getting interesting.

"Do you know his name?" I asked.

"Nope. Sorry. You'll find out soon, I'm sure."

Just then there was a knock at the front door. I ran to open it. It was Charity.

"Hi," she said as she stepped inside.

"Hi. Guess what? Did you see that moving van next door?"

She nodded.

"The new neighbor is a boy from our school."

"Who is it?" Charity asked.

"That's just it," I answered. "I don't know."

"Hmm, I wonder who it could be?" she asked. "What if it's Dave?"

"Or Spencer," I replied. We both smiled at the thought.

"How can we find out?" Charity asked. "We can't very well just hang around outside. That would be too obvious."

"I know where we can see," I said. "Let's go up to my room."

Charity followed me up the stairs to my bedroom. I looked out my window.

"Maybe we can see who it is from up here," I said. I could see some people, but they were quite a distance away. It was hard to tell who anybody was. "They're too far away," I said.

"Too bad we don't have binoculars," Charity remarked as she looked out the window.

"Hey, my dad has some," I said. "I think I know where they are, too. I'll go look."

I went into my parent's room and looked on the top shelf of my dad's closet. Hooray! We were in luck. There they were.

I hurried back into my room.

"I found them," I said.

"Oh, good," Charity replied. "Can I look through them first since it was my idea?"

"Sure," I answered as I held them out to her. "I really haven't used them very often. I'm not exactly sure how to adjust them so you can see."

"I know how to use binoculars," she said. "You just look through them and move this little bar right in front till it comes into focus. See?"

"We'd better lower the blinds so they can't see us looking out at them," I said as I put the blinds down.

"Yeah," Charity agreed. "It would be really embarrassing if they saw us up here." She poked the binoculars through a crack in the blinds and peered through them. "We should be able to see whoever it is pretty well through these."

"Are we being silly?" I asked.

"Nah, just curious."

"See anything?"

"Nope, just furniture—lots and lots of furniture," Charity answered.

Minutes ticked by and neither of us said anything.

"This is getting boring," I said finally.

"Oh, someone's coming. I see a car pulling up, but I can't see who's in it. Oh, good grief, they pulled into their garage."

"Let me look," I said, yanking the binoculars from her.

"Wait!" Charity yelled. "You're strangling me. Let me take them off first!"

"Oh, sorry," I said as she untangled herself and handed them to me.

I looked through them—it took a minute to get them adjusted. Not much to see. Nobody was there but the movers. Then a boy ran down the driveway to the truck for a minute and ran back to the house. I didn't get a good look at him, but he didn't seem to be anyone that I knew.

"I saw him," I said.

"Who is it?" Charity asked.

"I don't know. It's not anybody I know. Here, you look. You've lived around here forever. Maybe you'll know who he is."

Charity watched out the window for a few minutes, but the boy was gone. We waited patiently while she kept peering through the binoculars.

Finally, she spoke up. "I see somebody! Wait! He's out of focus. Let me try to adjust these. Now I see him. Who is that? Wait a minute . . . no, no, it can't be . . ."

"Who is it?" I practically shouted.

Charity looked absolutely forlorn and slumped down until she was sitting on the floor. She leaned against the wall and kept shaking her head, mumbling, "No, it can't be."

"I'm going crazy, Charity. Tell me what's wrong," I said.

"Oh, Britt," she said, finally. "It's worse than I ever imagined. Do you know who it is? Do you know who moved in next door to you?"

I shook my head.

"It's Mickey . . . Mickey the Creep."

"Mickey the who?" I asked as I took the binoculars and focused on a short, red-haired boy.

"Mickey the Creep. The most annoying, most disgusting, absolute biggest brat in the whole world just moved in next door to you. Oh, Brittany, I hope it isn't true. I hope for your sake that he's just visiting. If not, I feel really sorry for you. I feel sorry for both of us. Mickey has been in my class every year since kindergarten. He pulls all kinds of pranks all the time. He loves to tease anybody and everybody. He is the absolute worst."

Just as she was saying that, I looked out the window and watched Mickey as he yanked a skateboard out of one of the boxes. He leaped on it and rolled down the sidewalk.

One of the movers had to jump out of the way to keep from getting run over. The mover turned around angrily and yelled after him, but it didn't seem to matter to Mickey. He just laughed and kept going. From the looks of it, it seemed as if everything Charity just told me about this boy was true.

Charity and I trudged downstairs as if we were marching to our doom. My mother was busy working at her desk.

"What are you doing?" I asked. "Why are you working on a Saturday?"

"I've gotten so far behind in my work lately," she replied. "I thought I'd try to catch up a little. I can tell from the expressions on your faces that something absolutely dreadful has happened. What kind of earth-shattering event has occurred now?"

"Nothing much," I replied sarcastically, "except if what Charity says is true, my life is over."

"It can't possibly be that bad, can it?" my mother asked.

"Oh, yes it can," Charity complained. "The worst possible boy in the whole world just moved in next door."

"Oh my," my mom went on. "Really? Well, I hope it won't be as bad as you think." I could tell my mother didn't quite believe what we were saying. She seemed to want to get back to her work. So Charity and I went out the back door to the patio and sat down at the picnic table.

"How come parents never seem to believe it when kids try to tell them stuff?" I asked.

"Beats me," Charity shrugged. "It's like it's some kind of law or something. I wonder how long it will be before Mickey pulls one of his wonderful little pranks?"

As if on cue, a shower of water came spraying down over our heads.

"What was that?" I yelled as we ran for shelter.

"Well, it's not raining, that's for sure," Charity angrily replied. She looked over in the direction where the water came from.

"I knew it," she said.

"What?"

"I saw his ugly red head next to the fence. Come on."

Charity jumped up from the table and took off toward Mickey's house with me tailing right behind.

"This is war," she said.

She went through the gate and rounded the fence on his side.

Suddenly, there he was. I got my first close look at Mickey the Creep.

"Okay, Mickey, this is it. You might as well knock it off right now," Charity demanded.

Mickey looked up at Charity. He was considerably shorter than she was. He had wild red hair that curled like springs on his head and more freckles than I'd ever seen on one person.

He half-smiled, half-sneered, his beady brown eyes gleaming. "Oh, I'm so scared, Charity. What are you going to do?"

"I'm going to tell your parents that you sprayed us with the hose. That's what!"

"Oh, was that you? So sorry. I was just watering the yard. I guess I didn't see you over there," he replied sarcastically. "Go tattle to your mommy. I don't care. Nobody'll do anything."

"Tell me it isn't true," Charity went on angrily. "Tell me you don't live here. Tell me you're just visiting."

"Okay, I'll tell you I'm just visiting . . .," he said. Then he turned and stomped away, laughing. ". . . but it's not true. Hee-hee, ha-ha! Too bad for you."

Charity turned back to me, shaking her head, and said, "This is going to be no fun, Britt—no fun at all."

Three

Dᴜʀɪɴɢ the next few days, I found out how right Charity was. Mickey was a brat with a capital *B*. On Sunday afternoon, I went out in the backyard. It was an especially hot day for October, even in Florida. I had decided to go read my book outside. I sat down on the grass and leaned back against a tree, stretching my legs out to get comfortable.

I had been sitting out there for a while when, out of the corner of my eye, I saw something moving up and down . . . up, then down. I glanced over to where I thought it was, but there was nothing there—just a tall fence. So I went back to my reading. Then I saw something again, up and down, up and down. I glanced back again. Nothing there. What in the world was going on? It was hard to concentrate on my book. I kept glancing over toward the fence. This time I saw someone jumping on the other side—way up—higher than the six-foot fence. Someone with red hair. Who else? Mickey. I realized then that he had a trampoline. Oh, great.

"Hello, Ugly," he yelled over the fence as he was in midair. On the next jump, he stuck out his tongue.

I decided to ignore him and went back to my reading.

"Hey, Brittany, anybody ever tell you you've got the face of a saint?"

I tried to ignore him again.

"It's true, Brittany . . . a Saint Bernard!" He laughed loudly.

I shook my head and went back to my book. Unfortunately, I could still see him jumping up and down, up and down. I turned my head a little bit away from his direction. I figured if I just ignored him, he'd realize that it was no use and he'd just leave me alone.

"You know, Brittany," he started again, "on the day you were born, your father took one look at you and you know what he did?"

I pretended not to listen.

"He went to the zoo to throw rocks at the stork." Mickey roared with laughter.

At that point, I was trying very hard to act as if I was totally absorbed in my book. I was not going to let anyone as immature as Mickey get the best of me. I moved over a little so I was facing the other way. That way I didn't have to see him at all. Unluckily for me, I could still hear him.

"You know what, Brittany?"

Just keep reading, I told myself.

"You have a very striking face . . ."

Ignore him. Pretend you can't hear his stupid jokes.

". . . with a baseball bat, that is!"

That did it. I got up. I couldn't resist yelling one great insult as I stomped off into my house.

"Hey, Mickey, do me a favor. Move back to whatever zoo it is you came from," I called.

Just as I was saying that, my mother stepped outside.

"Brittany!" she said, horrified. "Who are you yelling at?"

"Him," I said, pointing over to where Mickey had been jumping on the trampoline. But, of course, the second my mother appeared, he stopped jumping. So she didn't see anything at all.

"Well, he was over there a minute ago," I said defensively.

"Brittany, I must say, I'm surprised at you. That's certainly no way to talk to one of our neighbors," my mother said.

"I suppose it's okay for him to call me ugly?" I asked.

"Oh, Brittany, don't you realize? Most of the time when boys say things like that, it's just because they want to get your attention," she went on. "He probably likes you."

I made a face. The thought of Mickey liking me was beyond disgusting. I opened my mouth to say something, but realized any discussion was probably useless.

"Never mind," I said, going inside. How long was I going to have to put up with this stuff?

The next day was Monday. My mother had an early doctor's appointment, so I had to ride the bus to school. Riding the bus usually wasn't too bad, but that was before you-know-who moved in next door.

I was standing at the bus stop, waiting and minding my own business, when Mickey and two of his sidekicks wandered over.

"Oh, look," he said. "It's what's-her-name. You know, Donation's friend."

"Ha-ha," his two buddies hooted. "That's a good name for Charity. Ha-ha, Donation!"

I glared at them. But before I could think of a worthy reply, the bus pulled up. I looked for an empty seat close to the driver. I figured that maybe Mickey would have to leave me alone then. Unfortunately, most of the seats were already filled. I finally found one in the middle of the bus.

We rode along normally for a couple of minutes. Then I felt something hit me in the back of the head. It landed on the seat next to me. It was a wadded-up piece of paper. I turned around but couldn't tell where it came from. I had a sneaking suspicion who the culprit was. As soon as I turned to face forward, another wad of paper hit me in the head. That made me angry. I knew it had to be Mickey, but, of course, he acted all innocent. I didn't want to have to complain to the driver. Mickey would just say that he didn't do it, and I'd wind up sounding like a whiny little baby.

I was glad when Charity stepped onto the bus.

"Hey, it's Donation!" Mickey yelled.

The bus driver told him to quiet down. Thank you, Mister Bus Driver.

As we rode to school, Charity sympathized with me about my Mickey problem.

"I understand," she said. "Remember, I was stuck in the same class with him for six years."

"*Six years*," I repeated. "I don't know how

you managed to keep from going totally loony. He hasn't even been living there for a week, and he's already driving me crazy. I just can't stand having him next door."

"Well, you have one thing to be thankful for," Charity replied. "At least you don't have to ride the bus with him every day since your mom drives you to school sometimes."

"Thank goodness for that," I agreed.

* * * * *

After school, I invited Charity to come over to my house so we could do homework together. We rode the school bus to my stop, and then we talked as we walked the rest of the way to my house.

As we got closer, Charity remarked, "Hey, Britt, isn't that your mother's car in the driveway?"

"She must have gotten off work early. I wonder how come?"

"You're home early," I said to my mother when we got inside.

"Hello, dear. Why, hello, Charity, how are you?" my mother asked. Then she turned to me. "Yes, I am home early. I'm going to be coming home early from now on. The doctor said I need to cut back on my hours."

"Why did he say that?" I asked.

"I've been a little stressed out, and my blood pressure is up. The doctor explained that it's nothing to worry about. I just need to take it a bit easier. So, from now on, I'm going to go in just a little earlier, and then come home by lunch time."

"Oh, good," I said. "You'll be home in the afternoon when I get home from school," I said, smiling.

"Yes, I will. But, you realize, of course, that we'll have to make one more change, don't you?" she asked.

"What?"

"Since I'm going in earlier, you'll have to continue riding the bus to school," she went on. "But that won't be so bad. Especially since Charity rides the same bus, right?" She smiled at Charity and went on. "You know, Brittany, you're very lucky to have found such a good friend since we moved here."

I nodded in agreement. I didn't want to bother telling her about Mickey being on the bus, especially if my mother had a problem that meant she needed rest. He might be a pest, but I would just have to find a way to handle it.

"Yeah, Charity's on the same bus," I replied. "It'll be fine."

As soon as we finished talking to my mother, Charity and I went upstairs to my room. I threw my backpack onto the floor and slumped down next to it. I was miserable.

"Well, now that my mother has some kind of a problem with her blood pressure," I said, "just call me 'Brittany Wilson—Bus Rider.'"

"Don't worry," Charity answered. "I'll sit with you every day. Besides, it won't be forever. Didn't you say the baby will be here in about four months?"

"True," I answered. "I guess that's not too bad."

Even though I said it, I didn't quite believe it. Four months seemed like forever.

"I know," Charity said. "I have an idea that will get your mind off this Mickey problem. Let's think up names for the baby."

"Names? I'm sure my parents will think of a name."

"Well, you'd better have some suggestions," she went on, "or the baby could end up with a name like mine." She rolled her eyes for emphasis. "Do you think for one minute that I would have picked a name like Charity if I'd had any say in it?"

I thought for a minute, then I said, "But I really like your name. It's so unusual. I don't like my name because it's too common."

"Well, that's the point," Charity explained. "We need to think of a name that's not overly unusual or too common. One that he or she is absolutely sure to like. Do you know what my parents almost named Molly?"

I shook my head.

"Ethel. They were going to name her Ethel," she said. "But I told them no way was any sister of mine going to have to go through life with a name like Ethel. Can you imagine? That's worse than Charity. They thought it over and picked the name Molly instead. Thank goodness."

"Gosh," I said, "there's more to this big sister stuff than I ever realized."

Charity nodded. "It's your responsibility to steer them away from names like Ethel."

"Or Mickey," I added.

"Definitely," Charity agreed.

So for the next hour or so, we sat in my room thinking of every possible name. Finally, we came up with two that we both liked— Amber for a girl and Ryan for a boy.

There was a knock at my door. It was my mom.

"Hey, you two want to go with me to the mall? I need to go look for some things for the baby."

We both nodded. "Sure," we said.

We got into the car with my mom, and she drove us to the mall. We parked beside a big store called Baby World.

As soon as we stepped through the door, I realized why it was called Baby World. It had everything, and I mean *everything*, imaginable for babies. Cribs, playpens, mobiles, diaper bags, bassinets, strollers, high chairs, swings . . . you name it.

"Wow," I said as I looked around in awe. "I never knew babies needed so much stuff."

"Gosh," Charity replied. "I don't think Molly ever had all this stuff."

"Well," my mother explained, "you don't really need all these things. Some of them just make life easier. Like a baby swing, for instance. When you were about six weeks old, Britt, that was the only thing that would put you to sleep. When the new baby comes, I'll definitely want another one."

We looked around some more. Tiny clothes, little bitty shoes—I never realized exactly how small a newborn baby is.

"You know, Brittany," my mother said, "I don't have much of anything left from when you were little. It's just like starting all over again. Of course, some of this baby stuff is so different now. We'll come back sometime, all of us, including your dad. We have to decide on a color for the baby's room first. Then we'll pick out everything. It'll be fun."

We walked around a little more.

When my mother walked ahead of us down one of the aisles, Charity whispered to me, "I have an idea. Why don't we ask my mom if we can give your mother a baby shower? You and I can plan it. It would be so cool, Britt."

"Wow, that would be neat," I replied. "How would we know who to invite?"

"My mom would know," she went on. "Your mother's gotten to know a lot of people by working on the committees at school and working at the community garden."

"Okay," I said. "We'll see if we can do it."

"Let's go to my house later," Charity said. "We can ask my mom together. But I know she'll say it's a great idea. She loves that kind of stuff. Don't say anything to your mother, though. It has to be a surprise."

*　　　*　　　*　　　*　　　*

Charity and I were so anxious to find out if we could go ahead with the baby shower that we headed to my house as soon as we could. When we got there, Charity's mother was sitting in front of a huge, wooden roll-top desk in their den.

"Hey, Mom," Charity said right away, "Brittany and I had an idea."

"Is it an idea I'll like?" her mother asked, looking up from what she was working on.

"I can't think of any reason that you wouldn't," Charity replied.

"Sounds good so far," she said, joking.

"Well, remember I told you about Brittany's mom having a baby, right?"

"Right," her mother answered. "By the way, congratulations on becoming a big sister, Brittany."

I smiled. "Thanks," I said.

"Well," Charity continued, "we went to a store with Brittany's mom today and looked at baby stuff. Her mom said that she doesn't really have anything left from when Brittany was a baby. She said it was like starting all over again. So I thought maybe we could give her a surprise baby shower."

Her mother didn't have to think long about it before she said, "Why, Charity, that's a great idea. I love it."

Charity turned to me and whispered, "I told you."

"In fact," her mom went on, "I just saw the cutest idea for a baby shower cake. A garden cake with little babies sitting among the flowers and vegetables."

"Cool," I said. "My mom would love that. You know how she's gotten involved with the community garden. That would be perfect."

"Maybe we could decorate everything to look like a baby garden," Charity said.

"We should make that the theme," Mrs. McKay continued.

"When would we have it? Could we have it soon?" I asked.

"I don't see why not," Mrs. McKay replied.

Charity and I did a little cheer. "Yeah!" we shouted.

"A baby!" Zach chirped from the corner of the room where he was sitting surrounded by building toys. He looked cute with his shaggy brown bangs and his baggy overalls. "Who wants a dumb old baby? Yuck!"

"Zachary," Charity responded, "you are not part of this conversation."

Zachary went on talking anyway. "Did you know that some animal babies are able to stand up just a few minutes after they're born? Horses and buffalo . . . and giraffes can, too. And did you know that a newborn giraffe is about six feet tall?"

"I don't think we have to worry about a six-foot-tall baby, Zach," I said, laughing.

Zach kept on talking. "Most animals are born knowing some things. That's called instinct."

Charity shook her head and sighed loudly. Then she motioned for me to follow her up to her room. "Come on, we'll make plans," she said.

We went to her room and sat down on her antique bed. Charity grabbed some notebook paper and pens, and we worked on a list of stuff to buy.

"Let's see, my mom will probably take care of the invitations for us. But we'll need to buy some things." Charity read off the list. "Decorations, balloons, streamers, a table-cloth, napkins, cups, paper plates, a cake . . ."

"How about a centerpiece?" I asked. "You know, something cute for the table. Maybe we can make one?"

"Yeah, but what?"

"Well," I went on, "our theme is a baby garden, so how about a basket of flowers with baby junk in it?"

"Baby junk?"

"Yeah, you know, bottles and pacifiers . . . baby junk."

"Oh," Charity said, "I know! I saw a center-piece from a bridal shower and they did something like that. They rolled up little hand towels to look like flowers."

"We could use some bibs and diapers," I added.

"This is going to be so neat," Charity said, smiling.

Charity and I spent the rest of the afternoon making plans and lists. We even drew a picture of the centerpiece so we would know what to buy when we went to the store.

When we were finished, we started walking back to my house. We took the lists and papers with us. We were so busy talking and comparing notes that we didn't even see Mickey sneaking up on us.

Suddenly, a hand came up beside me and grabbed the papers out of my hand. Mickey shoved us from his bike, laughing hysterically as he rode down the street waving the papers.

"Ahh-hh!" Charity yelled as she stumbled onto the grass and fell alongside the sidewalk.

I turned to make sure Charity was okay, and then I took off running after Mickey.

"Give me that!" I yelled.

"Well, gee!" he yelled back. "Guess I want to see what it is first."

"It's mine and I want it back!"

I kept running, but he stayed ahead on the bike. There was no way I'd catch up on foot, so I finally stopped.

Mickey stopped then, too, and goaded me on by holding the papers up like a flag. "Oh, let's see what it says. A baby shower— awwww, how sweet."

"Give them back to me, Mickey," I said as I started marching solidly toward him.

"And a pretty little picture, too," he went on. "Except it looks like some kind of alien."

"It's for my mother, so give it to me," I demanded.

"Did you say it's your mother? Is your mother an alien?" he added sarcastically. Then he took the lists and drawings, crumpled them all up, and threw them at me as he took off down the street on his bike.

I picked up our carefully made lists. I was so mad! Our hard work looked like pieces of trash. We'd have to copy everything over. I tried to smooth them out as best I could. Then I walked back to where Charity was standing up, brushing herself off.

I couldn't help but think about how Mickey always managed to spoil our fun. Was this how it was going to be from now on? Was Mickey the Creep always going to make my life miserable?

Four

FOR the next couple of weeks, Mickey did his best to drive me crazy. Since he moved in, my neighborhood had become a war zone. Whenever I walked out the door, I was prepared to duck flying missiles. It made me mad. After all, I should be able to relax a little in my own backyard.

On Monday, as Charity and I rode the bus home after school, it was more of the same. Before we'd gone even two blocks, Mickey had hit us with half a dozen rubber bands.

I turned to Charity. "We've got to think of something. I hate having to put up with this."

"I know what you mean," she replied, and turned to glare at Mickey.

"Should I tell his parents about the things he's been doing?" I asked.

"Well, you can try, but I'll tell you right now that his dad travels a lot, so he's hardly ever home. And as for his mother, well, have you met her yet?"

"No," I said, shaking my head.

"It's hard to explain. Let's just say she's different. She thinks Mickey is a perfect angel. You'll understand when you meet her."

"Well, I really don't want to worry my parents about all this right now," I said. "I mean, I don't want to be responsible for stressing my mom out, especially since the doctor told her to take it easy."

"I know what you mean," Charity replied. "But it's obvious that sooner or later, we'll have to do something."

"That's for sure," I said. "I feel like I'm living in one of those old monster movies. When you least expect it—WHAMMO!"

The bus arrived at school, and we waited together until the bell rang. Then we walked to our lockers together. We were halfway down the hall when I realized that something about my locker looked different.

As we got closer, I shrieked, "Oh, no, my locker's wide open, and my books are all over the place!"

"I'll help you, Brittany," Charity said, as she tried to quickly pick up my scattered books and papers. The halls were very crowded with students on their way to first period.

Even though they didn't mean to do it, the kids kept stepping on my books and kicking them around. Finally, when most of the kids were in their classrooms, Charity and I were able to retrieve my books. I counted them to see if I had everything.

"Okay, I've got my notebook, my folders, science book, math— I'm missing reading and English."

"Here, I've got them," Charity said, handing them to me. "Oh, look at your notebook, Britt. It's ruined."

My poor notebook was bent and half-crushed, a big footprint on the cover.

"How did this happen? How did my stuff end up all over the place?" I asked.

"Could you have left the locker open by mistake?"

"I don't think so because I remember clicking the lock shut," I answered.

"How else could it have been opened?" asked Charity.

"I don't know. How would anybody know my combination? Besides, it looks like someone purposely threw everything all over the place. You don't think it could possibly have been Mickey, do you?"

"I don't know, but I wouldn't put anything past him. I know what we'll do," Charity said.

"Why don't you put your books in my locker for now? At least they'll be safe for the time being."

"Good idea," I replied. "Think you'll have enough room?"

"We'll make room!"

"Should we tell someone what he did?" I asked.

"We've got no way to prove it was Mickey," Charity replied.

The bell rang and it was time for us to get to our classes.

"See you at lunch," Charity said as we went our separate ways.

Later, when the bell rang signaling lunch period, Charity and I returned to her locker to get our lunch bags.

"Think it's safe to go back to my locker?" I asked.

"I don't trust him," she said.

"Well, I don't trust Mickey either, but we don't really know if he did it."

"True," she answered, "but *somebody* did."

While she was unlocking the locker, I asked, "Charity, do you smell something?"

"Yeah, something smells funny."

As soon as we opened the locker, we saw what it was. Someone had sprayed shaving cream through the vent holes of the locker.

Huge globs of shaving cream dripped off our lunch bags onto our books stacked underneath.

"Y-u-u-c-k!" Charity screeched.

I picked up my soggy lunch sack. I opened it up and took out the sandwich.

"It's ruined," I said.

"Yeah, it all smells like shaving cream," she replied.

"So what do we do now?" I asked.

Charity shook her head at the mess. "I guess we clean this up, and then we buy our lunch today."

It took us quite a while and a lot of paper towels to get Charity's locker cleaned up. We washed the books off as best we could, but they still smelled funny.

I had plenty of money for both of us to buy lunch. When we finally sat down at our usual table, Charity could see that I was really mad.

"I'm going to tell Mickey to knock it off," I said.

"How do we know for sure that he was the one who did it?" Charity asked.

"Well, he's sitting right over there," I replied. "Let's pretend that we know it was him for sure. Maybe we can trick him into admitting it."

I jumped up from the table and marched over to Mickey and his buddies. Charity followed right behind me.

"Guess you think your little trick was pretty cute, huh?" I asked angrily.

"Well, I know you think I'm cute," he sneered, "but I don't know what little trick you're talking about." His friends all laughed.

"You know exactly what I'm talking about," I replied. "And I can prove that it was you."

Mickey paused and thought about that for a minute. Then he laughed again. "You can't prove anything," he said.

I was fuming, but I didn't know what else to say.

Finally, Charity spoke up, "Leave us alone, and leave our lockers alone."

We started to walk back to our table.

Mickey yelled after us, "Hey, Brittany! Speaking of tricks—have you taught Charity to roll over yet?" The boys all hooted and clapped at that one. It was embarrassing. Everyone around there heard Mickey make a joke out of us.

"Did you hear how he answered me? How he said that we couldn't prove anything?" I asked.

"Yeah," she answered. "He sure sounded like he knew what we were talking about, though, didn't he?"

"Exactly," I agreed.

"What are we going to do now?" I asked Charity when we sat back down.

"We'll go talk to the assistant principal. Maybe he'll talk to Mickey. Other than that, I don't know," she said, shaking her head.

We had a short meeting with the assistant principal right after lunch. He said he would bring Mickey in and get his side of the story. I was not convinced that anything would change.

When school was out, Charity and I rode the bus home together. Charity said good-bye and got off at her bus stop. Then it was my turn. I was anxious to get into the safety of my house. I hurried down the sidewalk, staying as far away from Mickey as I possibly could. I opened the front door and felt a sense of relief. I threw my backpack onto the floor and yelled, "Mom, you home?"

"In the kitchen, dear," she answered. I could hear conversation, so I knew she wasn't alone.

When I stepped into the kitchen, I saw a woman who had what Charity would call "big hair" sitting at the table with my mother. Not only was it big, it was very, very red. She had on a blazing orange dress, a lot of bright blue eye shadow, and too much lipstick. As I stood there, I couldn't help but think that something about this woman looked familiar.

"Brittany," my mother said, gesturing toward the woman, "this is Mrs. Rudolf, our new neighbor."

"Oh," I replied, "you must be Mickey the Cr—uh, I mean, uh, you're Mickey's mother."

"Why, yes, dear," Mrs. Rudolf confirmed with a wide grin. Then she yanked me over and wrapped one of her huge arms around me. "I guess you've met my sweet little Mickey."

I was pretty much speechless at this point, so I simply nodded.

She went on, laughing loudly as she kept me in a bear-like squeeze. "I suppose I'm biased, being that I'm his mother, but Mickey is just such a darling boy. He's so kind and considerate, a wonderful child. I expect that you two will become the best of friends." She smiled at me, then turned to my mother and added, "Why, who knows, Brittany and Mickey might end up being sweethearts."

I gasped. I was horrified at the thought. Mickey the Creep and *me?* He might be his mother's sweetheart, but he certainly would never be mine. I wanted to escape from this annoying woman as quickly as possible. I could see what Charity meant about his mother.

I was as polite as I could stand to be, considering the situation. I nodded and said, "Nice to meet you, Mrs. Rudolf." Then I somehow managed to untangle myself from her grasp and bolted up the stairs to the safety of my room.

*   *   *   *   *

Day after day, Charity and I kept hoping that Mickey would get into big trouble, but he never did. No matter what he did, he always managed to get away with it. At least he left our lockers alone. Maybe the assistant principal had scared him. But we couldn't waste time worrying about Mickey. We were too busy planning and buying things for the surprise baby shower.

I had somehow managed to keep the baby shower a secret from my mother, but it wasn't easy. I almost gave it away once when my mom was looking through a catalog of baby items. She pointed out one of the baby swings.

"This looks like a nice design," she said, showing it to me.

"Yeah, that one's neat," I replied. I smiled

to myself, knowing that Charity and her mother had bought one exactly like it for my mother.

"I definitely need to get one of those before the baby comes," she added with emphasis.

"Well, you'll have one pretty soon," I replied without thinking. Whoops!

"Huh?" she looked puzzled.

"Er . . . uh . . ." I stammered. "I mean, we'll be buying one before you know it."

She smiled then and didn't seem to notice anything peculiar about what I'd just said.

Whew! That was *too* close.

The next challenge Charity and I faced was figuring out a fool-proof excuse to get my mother to Charity's house on the day of the big event. Charity eventually came up with a good idea.

"I know," she said. "We'll have my mom call your mom and tell her that there's a meeting of the school improvement committee at our house on Saturday afternoon. That way she won't get suspicious when she drives up and sees a bunch of cars at our house."

I nodded my approval and said, "Works for me!"

One Friday night a couple of weeks before the shower, Charity and I decided to go pick out decorations. Afterward, I was going to sleep over at her house so we could work on everything together. Charity's dad dropped us off at the mall, and we went into an enormous store that sold party supplies.

"Boy, this store must have everything in the world for parties," I said as I looked around.

"Okay, let's see. We need to decide on colors first, right?" Charity asked.

"Yeah," I said. "So I guess we should get pink and blue. That way we can't miss. You know, pink for a girl and blue for a boy."

"Do we have to?" Charity asked. "That's what everybody gets. It's too ordinary!"

"So what would you suggest?"

"Let's look around for a while first."

I agreed. We ended up spending more than an hour walking up and down the aisles. There were so many colors. Creative Charity was never satisfied.

"I like the colors teal and purple," I said.

"But you have to admit that they really don't go with the theme of a baby garden," Charity replied.

Finally, we decided on light green and pale yellow with a little pink and lavender. We bought light green crepe-paper streamers to make the vines and leaves in a garden. Then we picked out pale yellow, pink, and lavender balloons. We decided to make matching paper flowers to go with the balloons.

Charity's mother had showed us the pretty glasses and plates she had selected, as well as a tablecloth that we could use. She felt that using paper plates, cups, and table covers was wasteful.

We paid for our stuff, then went next door to Baby World. Charity's mother had given us some money to purchase a few cloth diapers, washcloths, and bibs that we could roll up to look like roses.

"My mother loved the idea that the centerpiece will be as useful as it is pretty," Charity explained. "She found a basket for us to use and said that she'd help us arrange it so it looked nice."

After we paid for everything, we waited until Charity's dad picked us up and drove us back to their house.

When we got there, we put our stuff on the kitchen table and went upstairs to Charity's room. Her mother was getting Molly and Zach ready for bed. Zach was running around in Superman pajamas, wearing Molly's hooded baby towel as a cape.

"Look! Up in the sky. It's Superman!" he yelled as he ran down the hall with the towel flying behind him.

"Zach! I need that towel right this minute," Mrs. McKay called from the bathroom where she was bathing Molly.

Zach scampered back to the bathroom and reluctantly tossed the towel to his mother.

"How can I keep the world safe from evil villains if you keep taking away my cape?" he complained to his mother.

A few minutes later, Molly emerged looking like a little angel. Her blond hair was damp and curled softly around her face. She had on a long, flannel nightgown trimmed with ribbons and lace. She was wearing fuzzy pink bunny slippers.

"Aw-w-w," I said when I saw her. "She's so cute. I can't wait till I'm a big sister."

"You say that now," Charity replied as we went into her room, "but wait till the baby's here. I mean, I love my brother and sister, but they drive me crazy sometimes."

Charity went on, sounding like the resident expert. "Let me tell you what it's like when the new baby comes home. At first, the baby cries all the time, and everybody tiptoes around, afraid they'll wake it up. 'Be quiet, the baby is sleeping' is all you ever hear, over and over. Of course, the other big deal is germs. Everybody is constantly washing everything. 'Don't touch the baby till you wash your hands.' 'Don't give that to the baby till we wash it off' and on and on. But don't worry. It won't last forever. Sometimes I think Zach could eat dirt now and nobody would notice."

"I don't care if I have to be quiet all the time and wash everything in the whole house," I replied somewhat defensively. "It'll be my brother or sister and that's all that matters to me."

Mrs. McKay tucked Molly and Zach into their beds. Then the three of us went downstairs to the kitchen where we set up our work area.

We tried different ways to roll the bibs and other stuff to look like roses. Then Charity showed me how to make paper flowers out of pastel-colored tissue paper. Finally, we taped a flower rattle to the handle of the basket. The centerpiece looked great.

"I think it's going to be the most beautiful shower ever," I said.

Five

THE big day finally arrived—the day of the baby shower. I was so nervous. I wanted everything to be absolutely perfect.

I hurried over to Charity's house as early as I could. We had a lot of work to do.

"Come look at the cake," Charity said as soon as she opened the door. "My mother worked on it till late last night."

We went straight into the kitchen.

"Oh, it's adorable," I said admiringly as soon as I saw it. The sheet cake was frosted with chocolate icing. In the middle was a green "garden" with rows of flowers and vegetables—little cabbages and carrots. Tiny plastic sleeping babies were curled among the vegetables and flower petals. My mother was going to love it!

As soon as we finished admiring the cake, we set to work decorating the house. We hung the crepe-paper streamers above the dining room table and twisted them to flare out to the corners of the room. After we finished with the streamers, we blew up the balloons and hung them around the room and then added the paper flowers that we'd made. Everything was going well—until Zach came along.

"Party!" he bellowed as he yanked down a couple of the streamers.

"Leave everything alone, Zach," Charity demanded. "Brittany and I have a lot to do."

"Happy New Year!" he yelled as he tossed the balloons up in the air.

"Mom!" Charity called. "Zach's wrecking the party stuff."

Mrs. McKay quickly appeared, grabbed Zach by the arm, and escorted him into the kitchen where she could keep an eye on him.

Finally, we were ready to decorate the table. We put the tablecloth on and then put the centerpiece in the middle. It was so pretty.

"Wow!" Mrs. McKay said when she saw the room. "You two outdid yourselves. Everything looks great."

"Thanks," we answered in unison.

We helped her bring out the plates, cups, and silverware. Then Charity and I went up to her room to finish getting ready. It was almost time for the big surprise.

"How do I look?" I asked her. Charity and I both had gotten something new to wear to the party. I twirled around, modeling my sweater and new jeans.

"Really nice," Charity replied.

"You, too," I said. I looked anxiously out the window. "It's almost time and I'm getting so nervous."

"Me, too," she replied. "But it's going to be okay. You'll see."

Just then the doorbell rang. Our first guests had arrived. We went downstairs. In no time, the living room was filled with my mother's friends and co-workers.

Charity said, "I have an idea that will keep Zach out of our hair for a while. Hey, Zachary, come here."

Zach walked over to where Charity and I were standing.

"Think you could be the lookout?" Charity asked him. "You know, tell us when Brittany's mother gets here?"

Zach's face lit up with excitement.

"Sure!" he said. Then he turned around and ran up the stairs. Charity shrugged. We didn't know what he could be doing up there—until he reappeared in his "spy" clothes: an oversized trench coat, a hat, and dark glasses.

"Sherlock Zachary Holmes—at your service!" he said.

Charity sighed, "Oh, brother! Zachary, are you going to be able to do this? You can't be obvious out there or she'll wonder what's going on."

"Have no fear—Sherlock Zachary Holmes has a plan. I'm going up in the old treehouse. When you see me wave the red flag, it means I see her car." He demonstrated by waving a red flag right in front of our faces.

We tried not to laugh.

"Okay," Charity said. "We're counting on you, Zach. Keep alert out there."

"Aye-aye, Captain," Zachary replied with a little salute. Then he ran out the door, straight to the treehouse.

Charity and I sat by the window and watched for his signal.

All of a sudden, there it was—the red flag.

"She's coming!" I yelled.

"Everyone get in their places," Charity directed.

Mrs. McKay shut the blinds so my mother wouldn't be able to see us from the porch.

The doorbell chimed.

Mrs. McKay opened the door while Charity and I stood right behind her.

"Surprise!" we all shouted.

"Oh my goodness!" my mother exclaimed in disbelief. "I had no idea." Then she laughed. "So this is my committee meeting, huh?"

Everyone laughed.

The shower turned out to be a big success. First, we played party games that Charity's mom said were typical for a baby shower. Then it was time for cake. We managed to take some pictures of it—just before Molly stuck her hand into the middle and pulled off two of the plastic babies.

"*My* babies!" she screamed. When we tried to take them from her, she ran down the hall.

"Just let her have them," my mother told us. "It's okay."

"We're ready to eat the cake now, anyway," Mrs. McKay agreed.

At last, it was time to open presents. I couldn't get over how cute baby stuff was.

My mother unwrapped tiny little sleepers and eensy-weensy little socks. Towels, sheets, diapers, toys. Then she opened a big box. It was the swing from Mrs. McKay.

"Just what I needed," my mother said, smiling with approval.

That's when I rolled in the biggest gift of all. It was from my father and me—a beautiful, lacy bassinet.

"Oh, Brittany," my mother gushed, "it's

gorgeous!" She hugged me tightly and brushed away a tear.

A little while later, the party officially ended. My mother thanked everyone as they left. We carried her presents out to our car. Then we helped clean up.

"We did it!" I said to Charity as I stacked cake plates to take into the kitchen.

"We sure did," she added with a smile. "And it turned out great!"

Six

THE time passed quickly. Thanksgiving came and went. Christmas was almost here. Our excitement about the baby was growing constantly. Our family continued to get things ready.

My parents had the baby's room painted a pretty shade of pale yellow. Then we all went together one day and picked out furniture—a crib, a dresser, a rocker, and a changing table. My mother and I picked out crib bedding that was decorated with fluffy little lambs. Everything looked adorable.

After we had it all set up, my mother and I put the things away that she'd gotten at the baby shower. As we did it, she had me help her take inventory of what we had and what we still needed to get.

"Let's see," she said, looking in the drawers. "We have only one set of crib sheets and two sets for the bassinet. We'll need lots more."

"How many?" I asked, holding my list.

"Probably at least five or six more sets of each," she answered.

"That many?"

"Babies wet a lot of sheets," she explained.

We went through everything—towels, diapers, undershirts, gowns. It was fun, and I loved helping her. It made me feel very grown up.

My mother really looked like she was going to have a baby. She kind of waddled everywhere she went. It didn't seem possible that there were just a couple more months to go. I couldn't wait. The doctor told my mother that my little brother or sister would be here just before Valentine's Day.

We finished our inventory, and my mother said she was going to go get off her feet for a while.

I headed out the front door to the mailbox to pick up the mail for her. BAM! I was hit on the back of my head with a water balloon.

"You idiot!" I yelled at Mickey as he ran back toward his house.

That was it. Whether his mother believed me or not, I was going to show her exactly what her son had done. I marched up to the door and rang the bell.

"Yes?" Mrs. Rudolf said when she came to the door.

"Mrs. Rudolf," I started, "your son just hit me in the head with a water balloon. Look at my shirt." I turned around to show her my wet clothing.

"Oh, really?" she answered coolly. "What exactly happened?"

"Well," I explained, "I was walking out to our mailbox, and he came up behind me and threw the balloon at me."

"So," she said, "he was behind you?"

"Yes," I answered.

"Well, then you didn't actually see him throw it at you, right?"

"Uh, no, but . . .," I added, "when I turned around, he was the only one there."

"Yes, dear," she went on wearily, "but, you didn't really see him. For all you know, someone else could have been with him. Some of these boys are so high-spirited, you see. Why, my dear, it could have been any one of a number of boys that I know."

"But, Mrs. Rudolf," I kept on, "I *know* it had to be Mickey."

"Well," she added, shaking her head, "if I see any of those other boys around, I'll have a word with them."

Then she shut the door in my face.

So much for getting any help from her.

I started walking back home to change my

clothes. It was a cool winter day, and here I was wearing wet clothes. Mickey stepped out from around the corner of his house where he had been hiding.

"Hey, Ugly," he yelled. "I saw your mother yesterday. She looks like a fat whale." He laughed loudly.

"Shut up, Mickey," I answered angrily. I wanted to go punch him in that big dumb face of his. I wanted to, but I didn't. Instead, I stomped home and slammed the door behind me.

"Brittany!" my mother spoke sharply from the sofa where she was resting. "What are you doing slamming the door like that? I practically jumped out of my skin." She'd been a bit edgy lately.

"Oh, sorry," I replied. "I was just mad about something."

"What?" she asked.

"Oh, it's nothing, Mom," I answered. She was supposed to be taking it easy on doctor's orders. I wasn't about to bother her about a dumb old water balloon.

I went upstairs to change my wet shirt before she noticed it.

"One of these days," I thought to myself, "I'm going to fix that stupid Mickey, if it's the last thing I do."

I called Charity and told her everything that had happened.

"Well, it doesn't sound like Mrs. Rudolf's going to be any help," she sympathized. "Not that I'm surprised."

"We've got to catch him in the act somehow, Charity, but what can we do?"

"Well," Charity replied, "I know someone we can ask for help."

"Who?" I asked.

"Who's the smartest person we know?"

"Heather the Brain," I answered.

"Who else?" she replied. "Let's talk to her at school tomorrow."

"It's worth a try," I agreed.

The next day at school, we waited for Heather outside the cafeteria. She's called The Brain for a reason—she's super-smart. Not only is Heather in really advanced classes, but she makes it all look so easy. Once when I needed help in math, she was assigned to me as a tutor. When she showed me how to do a problem, she did it so quickly, I couldn't believe it. She's that way in every subject. It's amazing. Some kids call her a nerd because of it, and maybe she is . . . at least a little bit. I mean, she wears big glasses, and she's kind of skinny anyway, so the glasses look even bigger on her. But, so what?

"Hi, Heather," I called to her as she walked by.

"Come sit with us today," Charity said.

"Sure," she answered.

Heather sat down at our table. I could tell she felt a little awkward. She kept fooling with her hair, brushing loose wisps behind her ears and tightening her ponytail. After a while, we started to talk. That's when Charity and I explained our problem.

"So, you see," I went on, "we want to find a way to catch him."

"Hmmm," Heather said and frowned a little in concentration, "that won't be easy."

I sighed with disappointment. I guess I had hoped that she would have some fabulous idea.

"But," Heather went on, "chances are he's going to get caught sooner or later. It's only logical."

"I hope so," I said.

"I hope so, too," Charity agreed. "For everybody's sake."

That's when I noticed that Charity was glaring at someone standing behind me. Who else?

"Hey, I see you've got a new friend," Mickey announced sarcastically. "Too bad she's even uglier than you two. Do you have eyes behind those owl glasses?"

"Get lost, Mickey," I said. I could see that Heather's feeling were hurt.

"Go look in the mirror, Mickey," Charity

taunted. "You're nothing to brag about."

"Don't feel bad, Heather," I said. "You know he says that stuff all the time."

"He didn't get the nickname The Creep for nothing," Charity added.

"It's okay," Heather replied. "I know that people like that are usually insecure about themselves."

"You are so right," Charity agreed. "Maybe he acts that way because he's so short.

"And you know what else she's right about?" I asked. "One of these days Mickey is going to do something to the wrong person. He'll get his. That's when we'll have our revenge."

* * * * *

Later that day when I got home from school, I saw my dad's car in the driveway. That was not normal.

"Hi, hon," he said as I opened the door. He looked worried.

"What's wrong?" I asked. I looked around. "Where's Mom?" I asked. I was worried.

"Don't be alarmed," my father said reassuringly.

"I knew it," I said. "Something's wrong. What? What is it?"

"Nothing's happened yet," he continued.

68

"That's why I came home to talk to you. Your mother had to go to the hospital. She's having a few problems, and they're going to keep her there for now."

"Why?" I asked anxiously. "What problems?"

"The doctors are worried that the baby might come early—that it could be premature. So they've put her in the hospital to try to prevent that from happening."

"Oh, no," I cried. "Will the baby be all right?"

"Like I said, Brittany," he went on, "nothing's happened yet. The baby is fine and healthy right now. That's why they're doing this. Please don't worry."

"But she's got almost two months to go yet. That sounds awfully early."

"Well," he said, "I'm not going to lie to you, Brittany. It *is* early, but we have every reason to believe the baby will be fine. I don't want you to worry."

"Can I go see Mom?" I asked.

"Sure, honey," Dad replied, "but not tonight. She needs to rest tonight. They've given her some medication, and it's made her very sleepy. We can go see her tomorrow, as soon as you get home from school."

"Do I have to go to school?" I asked. "I want to see Mom. What if something happens? I want to see her first thing in the morning."

"Nothing's going to happen," he insisted. "You have to go to school. This may go on for quite a long time. You can't miss two months of school. Don't worry. Your mom is in the best possible place right now. Every day that she can take it easy, the baby gets bigger and stronger. So we both have to be brave now. Everything will turn out fine."

I could feel my eyes welling up with tears. Dad put his arms around me and hugged me close.

"I want my baby brother or sister to be okay," I said, sobbing.

"So do we, honey," he said softly. "So do we."

Seven

THE next day at school, I couldn't concentrate on a thing. My father called the school counselor in the morning and explained to her about my mother. The counselor assured him that she would talk to my teachers and explain the situation.

Charity and Heather consoled me at lunch time.

"Everything will be okay, Brittany. I'm sure of it. You'll see," Charity said.

"That's right," Heather agreed. "Your mom has had the best of care. She'll be fine."

I gulped and nodded. I could feel the tears filling my eyes again. I didn't want anyone to see me cry. I quickly wiped my eyes. Then I took a bite of my sandwich. I could barely swallow it. It felt like a lump in my throat. It was so hard to think of anything else except my mom and the baby.

Charity could see how I was feeling and spoke up. "I bet you'll feel better later. Your dad said you could see your mom tonight. You'll feel better when you see for yourself that she's all right."

I nodded. She was probably right.

"That's true. I'll get to see her tonight," I agreed.

It made me feel a little better. We all sat together until the bell rang, and I actually managed to eat some of my lunch.

After school, Dad picked me up and took me straight to the hospital. I couldn't remember ever having been in a hospital before. My dad said that they took me to an emergency room once when I was a baby. I was sick and had a high fever and had to be checked by a doctor. Of course, I couldn't remember any of that.

The hospital was a bunch of huge, white buildings. We went in through the main entrance and walked down a maze of halls. Each hall had different-colored arrows pointing this way and that to help people from getting lost. Hospital workers in white coats walked by carrying clipboards and pushing carts. It was noisy and cold, and it smelled funny.

I felt even stranger when we got to my

mother's room and I saw her sitting there in a hospital bed. She was hooked up to all kinds of tubes and things.

"Hi, honey," she said.

At least she sounded okay.

"Hi," I answered quietly. I looked around the room. She had the room to herself. I could see our car in the parking lot from the window.

"Not much of a view, huh?" I said, trying to sound cheerful. Then I hesitantly asked, "How are you doing?"

"Fine," she answered. "Your dad said that he explained to you what was going on. Do you understand?"

I nodded.

"Well, everything is going well so far. So don't you worry about me."

"What is that tube in your arm?" I asked.

"That's an IV. That stands for intravenous. It's a way to give me medications or fluids. Most people get these when they're in the hospital. It's not anything bad."

"Oh good, I'm glad," I replied.

"So, tell me about your day at school."

"Okay," I said and proceeded to tell her about what went on that day.

After a while, it was time for us to leave. Dad and I gave Mom a kiss good-bye and said we'd see her tomorrow. I felt much better.

On the way out, we stopped and looked in the window of the nursery. In my whole life, I'd never seen so many babies in one place. All of them were lined up in a row of plastic bassinets. Some were crying; some were sleeping. They had all different colors of skin, from light to dark. Some had lots of hair. Some had no hair at all. And one little baby had hair that stood straight up on his head. Several nurses were tending to them, changing their diapers, and giving them water.

"Wow," I said as I gazed at all of them.

Dad said, "They're really something, aren't they?"

"They sure are," I agreed.

Maybe everything was really going to be fine after all.

*　　*　　*　　*　　*

After we left the hospital, Dad had some errands to run, so he dropped me off at Charity's house.

Charity met me at the door. We went up to her room and sat down on the floor.

I told her all about my visit to the hospital.

"It's kind of creepy there," I said. "It smells weird. And it's really noisy."

"I've been to the hospital before. When Zach was little, he got his finger caught in the door. They had to put a lot of stitches in it."

"Yuck," I replied.

"Yeah," she went on, "it was pretty gross. I remember he yelled a lot. When he came home, he had a bandage on his hand for a while."

Charity and I went downstairs, and her parents invited me to stay for dinner.

Charity's mother was very nice about everything. She explained that I shouldn't worry.

"Your mother has taken great care of herself. She'll do fine, you'll see," she said.

"You see!" Molly sang out from her high chair.

"I see you, Molly," Zach said. He peered at Molly with his hands cupped like binoculars.

"See me," she laughed shyly, as she covered her eyes with her hands.

One thing is for sure. Whenever I'm at Charity's house, Zach and Molly always manage to keep things lively.

We finished eating dinner and were cleaning off the table, when the phone rang. Mr. McKay answered it.

I didn't pay much attention, until I heard the serious tone of Mr. McKay's voice.

Especially when I heard him say, "Don't worry, we'll take good care of her."

Her? Was he talking about *me?*

When he got off the phone, he spoke to me quietly.

"Brittany, that was your father on the phone. He said that he has to go back to the hospital tonight. It seems that your mother has developed a few complications, and she wants him to be with her. Don't worry. He'll call us and let us know what's going on when he gets there."

Don't worry. Don't worry. If one more person told me not to worry, I was going to scream. How could I help but worry? It's my mother and my baby brother or sister they're talking about.

Charity wrapped her arm around my shoulder and said, "Let's go up to my room. I'll let you borrow a pair of my pajamas. Tomorrow's Saturday. No school. We'll have a slumber party."

She was trying to cheer me up, but it wasn't really working.

We went up to her room. I took a shower and put on her spare pajamas. Mr. McKay rolled a cot into Charity's room, and Mrs. McKay brought in sheets and blankets and pillows to make it comfortable for me.

76

Charity and I went downstairs to watch a movie, but my dad never called. Finally, I could barely keep my eyes open. So we went upstairs, climbed into our beds, and fell asleep.

I slept soundly through the night. I heard Charity get up in the morning, but I fell back to sleep. I woke up when she came back into the room to get dressed.

"Good morning, sleepyhead," she said, joking. "Rise and shine."

I yawned.

"I guess I must have been pretty tired," I said.

"I guess so," she said, laughing, and tossed a pillow at me.

I got up and went down to the kitchen. Her mother made me breakfast.

"Did my dad call?" I asked.

"No, hon," she answered, "not yet. But don't you worry."

There it was again. *Don't worry.*

"I'm sure he'll call soon. He probably just didn't want to wake us," she added.

I went back upstairs. Charity lent me some clothes, and I got dressed. The jeans were a little long for me, and I had to roll them up.

I heard the phone ring downstairs. I tried to listen to what they were saying.

"Brittany," Mr. McKay called. "It's your dad."

77

I went to the landing at the top of the stairs and stopped. My feet felt like they had lead weights on them.

"Brittany," he went on, "your mom's fine. But he wants to talk to you."

I scrambled down the stairs as fast as I could.

"Hi," I said. "What's going on, Dad?"

"Well, sweetie," he answered. "I've got some news for you. Mom had the baby last night."

My mouth dropped open. I couldn't think of anything to say.

Finally my dad asked, "Britt, are you still there?"

"I'm here," I said. "You're not joking, are you?"

"No, dear, I wouldn't joke about this. You have a little sister."

"A sister! A sister!" I was screaming so everyone could hear. "I have a little sister!"

Charity ran up and hugged me so hard I almost dropped the phone. Charity's whole family cheered. Even Shakespeare barked hurray!

"Brittany? *Brittany?*" My poor dad was still waiting on the line.

"Yeah, Dad, I'm here. I'm just so happy," I said finally. "When can I see her?"

"Now, just a minute," he went on. "I have more to tell you."

"What?"

"Well," he explained, "you have to realize that the baby is almost two months early. She's very tiny. Right now they have her in a neonatal intensive care unit."

"A what?" I asked. It sounded serious.

"They have her in a special place where they take care of all the premature babies. So far, so good."

"What do you mean, 'so far, so good'? You mean, she might not be okay?"

"She's doing very well for her size."

"Exactly how little is she?" I wanted to know.

"Your sister weighs three and a half pounds."

"Wow, that's pretty small, isn't it? Is Mom okay?" I asked. "When can I see my sister?"

"Yeah, the baby is pretty small, but she's doing well. Mom is fine. Just tired from being up most of the night. I need to run home and take a nap, too. You can't see the baby until tomorrow. All right?"

"All right. One more thing, Dad. Did you pick a name yet?"

"Yes, we did, Brittany. We decided that the name you picked out was just right. Your sister's name is Amber Rose."

"Neat, Dad. I can't wait to see her."

"I'll call you a little later, okay?"

We said good-bye and hung up.

I turned to Charity.

"Guess what?" I said. "They liked the name we picked. They're naming her Amber Rose."

"A sister," Charity replied. "Now we both have sisters—that's totally cool."

Mrs. McKay gave me a little hug.

"Congratulations, big sister," she said.

"Thanks," I said. "Wow! I can't believe that the baby's here already. Amber Rose."

"Yeah, big sister!" Charity added.

Eight

From the moment my father called, all I could think about was the fact that I had a sister. I couldn't even sit still, I was so excited. My father was going to stay with my mother at the hospital. I was so anxious to see Amber Rose.

Now that I knew I had a little sister, I really wanted to buy her something. I had some money my dad had given me earlier. Charity's mom said that she'd take us to the store.

"What should I get?" I asked Charity as we walked into the mall.

"What do you want to get?" she replied.

"Something very girlish," I answered. "I know. A dress. I want to buy her a dress."

"Back to Baby World," Charity said, laughing. "Seems like we've been spending a lot of time there lately, doesn't it?"

I agreed. "Yeah, and now that I have a baby sister, I'll probably be back a lot."

Once inside, we headed right to the girls' department.

"Wow, they have about a million baby dresses," Charity remarked.

"The sizes are weird," I added. "What in the world is a 2T?"

"T is for toddler," Charity explained. "I know that much from Molly. We need infant sizes. Here they are, the ones that go by months."

"Where do you find zero months?"

"It's not zero months. We look for the newborn size. See?" she pointed to the rack.

"Wow," I said. "These are so small."

We looked through the entire rack. Finally we picked one that was pale pink trimmed with little tiny rosebuds. Rosebuds for Amber Rose.

"Isn't it adorable?" I asked as we paid for it at the register.

"It sure is," Charity agreed. "You know, I'm so glad that we both have little sisters."

"Me, too."

After we got back to Charity's, she and I went up to her room and wrapped the gift.

"I'll take it to her today when I go to the hospital," I said.

"Maybe Amber can wear it when she

comes home."

"That would be neat," I agreed. "I wonder when she'll come home. Do you remember how long it was before Molly came home?"

"Not long. I think it was just a couple of days."

"I can't wait," I said.

Late that afternoon, my dad picked me up on his way back to the hospital. He had gone home for a quick shower.

When I got to the hospital, I found that Mom had been moved to a different room.

"Hi, Mom," I said.

"Hi, hon," she replied. She looked really tired. I gave her a hug.

"I can't wait to see the baby," I remarked.

"I bet you can't," my mother answered. Then she turned to my dad. "Did you explain to her about how the baby looks?" she asked.

"No, not really," he answered.

"Why?" I asked. "Is something wrong with the way she looks?"

"No, Brittany," my mother explained. "It's not that there's anything wrong with the way she looks. It's just that premature babies look a little different for a while."

"How?"

"They haven't had time to gain weight—so they're kind of skinny and tiny."

"And she's in an incubator right now," my dad continued. "So we haven't really been able to hold her much."

"Can I see her?" I asked again.

"We need to find out when you can see her," my dad answered. "I'll go talk to one of the nurses and see what I can find out."

I sat there keeping my mother company for a few minutes until my father came back.

He smiled. "Well, for right now, you can only see her through the window."

I sighed loudly with disappointment.

"I know that you were hoping to hold her. The nurse did say that you might be able to hold her for a few minutes in a couple of days. But you'll have to go through a little health screening first."

"Why is that?" I asked.

"They want to make sure that you're healthy. They can't risk exposing a tiny baby to certain things."

"I guess I can understand why that would be important," I agreed.

Dad and I visited with Mom for a few more minutes, but she was really tired, so we said goodnight.

Then we headed over to what they call the neonatal nursery. We waited in a special room for a few minutes until one of the nurses came in to talk to me.

"Hi," a tall, dark-haired nurse said as she stepped in. "My name is Kelly. I'm one of your new sister's nurses. You must be Brittany."

I smiled and nodded.

"Well, Brittany, you understand that your sister was born a little early. The reason we wanted to talk to you before you see your sister is to prepare you a little for exactly what a premature baby looks like. Has anyone explained anything about this yet?"

"My parents told me a little about it," I answered.

"Good. Well," she went on, "let me explain a little more. Right now your sister is in what we call an isolette. That's because premature babies sometimes have trouble keeping their body temperature stable. This way, we can keep your sister warm and keep a close eye on her. She also has some wires attached to her. These are monitors. It doesn't mean that there's anything wrong with her. They let us know how she is doing and they help us keep track of her breathing and her heart rate.

"But the first thing you'll probably notice when you see your sister is how small she is. That's because babies gain a lot of weight during the last couple of months before they're born. Your sister didn't have a chance to do that. But, don't worry, because that's very common in premature babies. She's really doing very well. So, what do you think—are you ready?"

I nodded. I was so nervous that I felt like my heart was about to burst. But I was more than ready—I couldn't wait.

My father and I followed the nurse out of the room. Kelly took us to a special window.

"This is our private viewing window for families," she explained. "I'll go in and tell them that you're ready to see her."

A couple of minutes later, one of the nurses inside the room pushed an isolette a little closer to the window. She pointed to the baby inside and turned it a little so we could get a good view.

There was my sister. She was so small— even smaller than I had pictured. I could see that she had dark hair that kind of stood straight up on top like a little mohawk. She was surrounded by so many tubes and wires—more than I imagined. She was dressed in just a diaper. She looked so frail. Her tiny little chest moved up and down with every breath. I was enchanted watching her. She stretched out one of her arms, and then one skinny little leg kicked. I couldn't take my eyes off her.

Finally my dad spoke. "So what do you think?"

"She's even tinier than I thought."

"That was my first reaction, too," he agreed.

"Is she going to be okay, Dad?"

"The doctors and nurses all keep telling me that she's doing fine so far."

"When can she come home?" I asked.

"Well, that's one question that we don't know the answer to yet," he said. "It depends on a lot of things, like how fast she gains weight. We'll just have to take it one day at a time."

One day at a time. All I knew is that I wanted my sister to be all right . . . and I wanted her to come home as soon as possible.

*   *   *   *   *

For the next couple of days, it seemed as if all the people in the whole world had their eyes glued to my baby sister—nurses, doctors, our family and friends—everyone.

When I went back to school the day after I saw her, I was so excited about everything. I couldn't stop talking about my new sister. Luckily, Heather and Charity were very patient with me about it.

87

But by Wednesday, their patience was beginning to wear thin.

"Did I tell you that Amber has this cute dark hair that sticks straight up on top of her head?" I asked.

"Yes, you just told me yesterday," Charity replied.

I looked over at Heather who nodded and quickly added, "And you told me this morning."

"Did I tell you that I might get to hold her soon?"

"Only about a zillion times," Charity said.

Heather nodded again.

Nobody said anything for a couple of minutes.

Finally I couldn't stand the silence any longer. "I don't know if I told you . . . you just couldn't believe how tiny she is."

"We know!" Charity and Heather chorused. Then they started laughing.

"You are hopeless," Charity went on, shaking her head at me.

When Dad picked me up after school that day, he had a big surprise. We were going straight to the hospital. I was finally going to get to hold Amber Rose.

"First, you'll have to go through that health screening that the nurse told you about," my dad cautioned as we drove over.

"I don't know what that means," I replied.

"Well, it means that they'll ask you some questions to make sure that you don't have anything contagious."

"Oh, I understand," I nodded. "Probably because the baby is so small, right?"

"Right."

When we got to the nursery, Nurse Kelly met us in the waiting room. We all sat down while she asked me and my dad some health questions—stuff like if I ever had chicken pox or the measles and if I had a sore throat today. Once she decided that I was healthy, she led us into the nursery.

"You'll have to wash your hands really, really well before you touch her," Nurse Kelly explained as she showed us the sink and the special soap. "And you'll have to put on a hospital gown and mask."

Dad and I scrubbed our hands several times, then Kelly handed us gowns and masks. We both laughed at the way we looked.

"Just call me Doctor Brittany," I said, joking.

"Look at me," Dad said. "I look like a burglar." We laughed some more.

As soon as we were ready, the nurse took us inside. My mother was already there. She was sitting in a rocking chair holding the baby. She looked just as funny with a mask on, but you could tell she was smiling. You could see it in her eyes.

Again, I was overwhelmed by how small my sister was. She was still attached to some tubes and wires.

The nurse took me over to another rocking chair next to my mom. Then she carefully picked up Amber Rose and laid her in my arms. As small as she looked before, she felt even smaller. I knew right away that the dress that Charity and I bought her would be much too big.

"Wow" was all I could whisper.

"She's tiny, isn't she?" my father asked as he knelt down next to me.

"Yeah, she is," I agreed. With her dark little mohawk, Amber didn't really look like any of my baby pictures. I had just a few wispy strands of blond hair when I was born. Suddenly, she opened her eyes and looked at me—they were dark blue, what my mother would call indigo. She stared up at me. It was almost as if she knew me. I touched one of her hands and her little fingers grasped mine and held on tightly. I smiled at her—my sister.

All too soon, it was time to go. Somewhat reluctantly, I handed the baby back to the nurse. My mother would be coming home the next morning—but not Amber.

"When can she come home?" I asked, practically pleading.

"She needs to gain some weight," my mother explained. "But it might not be too long. She's doing very well."

"Has she gained any weight yet?" I asked.

"No, honey, babies usually lose weight at first."

"Lose weight!" I replied with alarm. "She can't lose weight—she's so tiny already."

"She's not losing anymore," the nurse answered. "All babies lose weight at first. It doesn't mean that there's anything wrong."

"How long do you think it will be?" I asked again.

"Probably at least a month," my father replied.

I felt disappointed. A whole month. I was hoping that she'd be coming home soon before Christmas.

"We all want her home, Brittany," my father added, "but we want her to be healthy and strong and ready to come home. Right?"

I nodded.

After we visited with my mom for a while, Dad and I went back home. I was doing my homework when Charity called. I told her all about holding Amber for the first time.

"She's really beautiful," I said.

"I can't wait to see her," she replied.

"It'll probably be at least a whole month before she comes home, but my mom comes home tomorrow."

"Well, that's good, anyway," Charity replied reassuringly.

"Yeah, I mean I'm really glad that my mom will be home, but a month seems like such a long time, especially with Christmas coming."

"Yeah, I know. I bet you wish your sister could be home for Christmas. But look at it this way, at least you can be happy that she's doing so well."

"You know," I said, "we've been so busy with the baby and everything that I think we kind of forgot all about Christmas."

When I hung up the phone, I started to think about Christmas. It was going to be Amber's first one, and she would be spending it in the hospital.

That evening, Dad and I straightened up the house in preparation for my mom coming home. There was a mountain of laundry since nothing had been done for about a week. Together we tackled the laundry, until most of it was folded and put away. Mom was on strict orders to take it easy for a while. Dad said that she would probably be spending quite a bit of time at the hospital with the baby.

After we finished cleaning, I went up to the attic and looked for the boxes of Christmas decorations. I wouldn't be able to do it all myself, but I could at least make the house look a little more holiday-like. I carried down one box that contained odds and ends. I put some decorations over the mantle on the fireplace. Then I found the wreath and hung it on the front door.

In the bottom of the box, I found our Christmas stockings with our names on them. I hung them from the mantle. Three stockings—soon there would be four.

Suddenly, I had an idea.

"That's what I'm going to do," I said out loud. "Amber needs a Christmas stocking, too, and I'm going to get her one!"

Nine

MONDAY was school as usual—except that Charity didn't ride the bus in the morning. When I walked toward our usual table at lunch time, I noticed that Charity and Heather were already there—but I hardly recognized the table. It was decorated with balloons and a banner that read, "Congratulations, Big Sister!"

"We're giving you a Big Sister Shower," Charity explained happily.

"Wow!" I exclaimed. "When did you guys do all this?"

"We're pretty sneaky," Heather replied, smiling.

Two presents and a cake decorated with teddy bears were on the table.

"So this is why you didn't ride the bus this morning," I said to Charity. "I can't believe you did all this!" I shook my head in astonishment.

"Here," Heather said, handing me one of the gifts on the table. "It's from me. I hope you like it."

I was anxious to see what it was, so I tore off the wrapping paper. It was—what else from Heather?—a book.

"It's a book of nursery rhymes," Heather explained. "I wanted to get you something to read to Amber. I read in a magazine that reading nursery rhymes to small children helps them learn to read later on."

"Oh, thank you. I love it, Heather, I really do."

I could tell that Heather was happy that I liked her present.

Then I opened the present from Charity. Inside were two T-shirts—a big one for me and a matching little one for Amber. The big one read "I'm Amber's Big Sister" in bright colorful letters. And the little one read "I'm Brittany's Little Sister."

"Oh, Charity, I love them," I said as I held up the T-shirts.

"I'm glad," she replied, smiling.

"Did you make these?" I asked.

"Yeah, with a little help from my mom," she answered. "I know it's too big for her now, but she'll grow fast."

"Thank you both so much." I hugged each

95

of them. "You guys are the best friends anybody could have."

Charity and Heather smiled back.

"Should I cut the cake?" I asked.

"I thought you'd never ask," Heather answered. "I can't wait. It looks delicious."

Charity handed me some small plates, and I began cutting slices of cake for the three of us.

All too soon our happy moment was interrupted by—who else?

"Hey, how come you guys are having a party without me?" Mickey whined as he suddenly appeared next to the table.

"Get lost, Mickey," Charity insisted.

"But, Brittany, where's my piece of cake?" he went on.

"Go away, Mickey," I said.

I handed a plate to Heather and started cutting another one for Charity.

"Is that any way to talk to your next door neighbor?" he asked. Just then, he grabbed one of the pieces of cake and threw it at me. But I saw it coming and ducked.

The cake missed me completely. At first, I couldn't see where it landed. But I knew by the look on Mickey's face that something had happened. When I turned around, I saw that the piece of cake had hit someone in the back of the head—and that someone was Robert

Brown, the biggest, tallest, and toughest kid at Lakeside Middle.

It seemed as if everyone in the cafeteria stood still as Robert slowly rose from his seat. He shook the cake crumbs out of his hair and walked toward the spot where Mickey seemed to be frozen. Robert, who was at least six feet tall, towered over the trembling Mickey. He leaned down until they were eye-to-eye.

"You are dead," he threatened.

I thought to myself, *Boy, here it comes*. We knew that Mickey's luck would run out sooner or later. Now it finally had.

Mickey seemed to be shrinking before my very eyes. In fact, I don't think I've ever seen anyone look so scared in my entire life. With unblinking eyes, he watched Robert clench his hands into fists.

Then, for some strange reason—I don't know why I did it—I stood up and came to Mickey's defense.

"He didn't mean to do it, Robert," I said. "It was an accident."

Robert shifted his gaze to me.

"Some accident," he answered. "Maybe somebody else is going to have an accident," he went on as he turned his glare back to Mickey.

"Really," Charity backed me up. "It's the truth."

"Here, Robert," I said trying to think of some way to pacify him. "Maybe you won't feel so bad about wearing the cake if you can have some." I tried to be as friendly as I could. I cut a big piece of cake and held it out to him.

Robert didn't return the smile. He looked at the piece of cake I was handing him, and then looked back at Mickey.

Then he shook his head and kind of snarled to Mickey, "Ah, you're not worth it."

Apparently Robert had an appetite to match his size. He didn't say anything else, but he took the cake and sat back down at his table.

Mickey breathed a sigh of relief. He backed up a little and melted into his seat without saying another word.

Heather leaned over and spoke quietly to Charity and me, "I told you that sooner or later Mickey's luck would change."

"You were right," I said. "I just didn't know it was going to be so soon."

"Apparently, Mickey didn't either," Charity added.

As the lunch bell rang, I called out to Charity, "After school, I need to go to the store to buy something. Think your mom could take us?"

"I'll ask," she replied.

As it turned out, Charity's mother didn't mind, especially when I explained about wanting to get the baby a Christmas stocking.

"So where do we go?" Charity asked as her mother dropped us off.

"I'm not sure," I replied. "I want to find a stocking that matches the rest of our stockings if I can."

"That won't be hard," Charity remarked.

We found out that was not the case—six stores later! I just couldn't find a stocking that matched the rest of ours. I really wanted her stocking to look the same. We were a family now, and it was important to me.

"How about that stocking over there?" Charity asked, pointing to one behind the counter.

"No, it's too fuzzy on top," I said.

"We're running out of stores," she said, sighing.

"Let's just try a couple more," I said.

The next store had an entire aisle with nothing but stockings.

"If we don't find one here, I'm giving up," Charity insisted.

I started at one end of the aisle, and Charity started at the other. Every couple of minutes, Charity held up a stocking.

"Wrong color. Too short. Too long," I responded to her selections.

Then, "That's it! You found it!" I screamed.

"Good grief, calm down, Britt," Charity said, shaking her head.

"Hooray! Now Amber will have a stocking just like everyone else in our family," I said.

*   *   *   *   *

By the time I got home, it was already getting late. Who would have thought that it would take us almost three hours to find a Christmas stocking?

My mother was due to come home at any time. Charity's mother had stopped by the day before with some casseroles that we could keep in our freezer. That way we could just pop one into the oven for dinner. She said that she knew my mother was going to be tired for a while and that she'd be busy visiting the baby at the hospital every day. I took one of the casserole dishes out of the freezer and followed the directions for heating it up. I made a salad to go along with it and set the table.

Suddenly, there was a knock at the door.

I didn't think it was my parents because I didn't hear the car pull up. Besides, why would they knock? I looked out the window. It was Mickey. I debated whether to open the door or not, but my curiosity finally got the best of me.

I opened the door, but I didn't say hello. I simply stared at him, waiting for him to say what he wanted.

He stood there, not saying anything. He seemed embarrassed, just looking down at his feet. He held his hands behind his back and didn't look up. For a second, I was afraid that maybe he was hiding something to throw at me. Then, he took a package out from behind his back and thrust it at me.

"It's, uh, for the baby," he explained.

It was a present, awkwardly wrapped, obviously one that he had managed to do by himself. I opened it. It was a stuffed animal—a fluffy little white duck.

"Thank you," I said, not really knowing what else to say.

"Yeah, w-w-well, uh," he stammered as he finally looked up at me. "Thanks for speaking up for me today to, uh, to Robert, I mean."

I nodded.

"I, uh, I hope your sister does okay," he went on.

"Thanks," I said.

"Nobody knows . . . I mean, I never told

anybody, but," he said, looking back down at his feet, "I was premature, too."

Neither of us said anything for a minute. For one thing, I was absolutely speechless— Mickey, a premature baby. Who would've thought?

Then Mickey suddenly said "bye" and ran back toward his house.

I shook my head in amazement as I watched Mickey run away. I couldn't believe it. Not only had he said thank you, but he had actually brought a gift over for Amber, too.

"No one will ever believe what just happened," I said out loud.

I think I was still standing there dumbfounded when my parents' car pulled up in the driveway. My father got out and ran around the car to open the door for my mother. Slowly and carefully, she stood up and walked toward the house. She looked very tired. I rushed over to give her a gentle hug.

"I'm so glad you're home, Mom," I said.

"I'm happy to be home, dear," she said as we walked toward the front door.

That's when I noticed that my mother looked sad.

"What's wrong, Mom?" I asked.

"Mom's just feeling a little sad about having to leave Amber at the hospital," my dad explained.

"It was hard to leave her there," my mother added, tears filling her eyes. "She just looks so tiny and helpless."

"But, Mom," I spoke up as we went in and closed the door behind us, "remember what they told us. She's getting the very best care."

"That's right," Dad continued. "She's where she needs to be for now."

". . . and you'll see her tomorrow," I added.

". . . and she'll be home before you know it," Dad chorused.

"Oh, all right," Mom said. She laughed a little and then smiled. "I give up. You two are relentless."

"Something sure smells good," said Dad.

"I made dinner," I announced, feeling very grown-up. "But first I have to show you something."

I led the way over to the fireplace.

"You decorated the mantle," my mother said, noticing right away.

"See anything else?" I asked.

"Oh my, of course," my mother said happily. "Four stockings! You got Amber a stocking. Oh, look," she said to my father, "it even matches the rest of ours. You put her name on it, Brittany. How thoughtful."

My dad gave me a big hug and said, "I don't know when you managed to do all this. I have to say that Amber couldn't ask for a better big sister."

"I guess we really did kind of forget about Christmas, didn't we?" my mother remarked thoughtfully.

"Well, there's one way to take care of that," Dad replied. "How about Brittany and I go pick out a tree after dinner? What do you say?"

"I say yes!" I said, clapping.

"After all the work she's done, I think this is one big sister who deserves a tree," Mom agreed.

"She sure does," Dad replied.

"Thanks, Dad," I said proudly as I led the way to the dinner table.

As soon as we finished dinner and cleaned up, Dad and I took off to find a tree. We went to the little Christmas tree lot right up the street. It didn't take us very long to find a good one. We tied it to the roof of the car and headed back.

We made Mom comfortable on the sofa.

"We know you're tired, so you just take it easy," Dad said.

"Yeah, Mom," I said. "You can be the critic

and tell us what looks good."

Meanwhile Dad and I got busy hauling boxes from the attic into the living room. In no time at all, our Christmas decorating began to take shape.

"It looks like a regular winter wonderland," my mother said happily.

"It is starting to look pretty good, if I do say so myself," my father agreed.

"Hooray for Christmas!" I shouted.

Ten

THE morning of Amber's first Christmas was nothing like I thought it would be. How could it be when she couldn't be here with us? From the time my parents and I got up that morning, the day seemed rather depressing. We went through the motions of opening our presents, but we all acted as if we were in another world.

"You know," I said to them, "I don't really feel like celebrating."

"I know what you mean," my mother agreed. "I think it's because we know that Amber can't be here with us yet."

"Yeah," I said. "It feels like something's missing."

"Or someone," my father added.

"I can't stand being here away from her," I said.

"Neither can I," my mother agreed. "Let's

get ready and go to the hospital right now."

As soon as she said that, we all jumped up and got ready in record time. By the time we were on our way to the hospital, we were all in a much more cheerful mood.

The hospital looked different to me these days—not as cold or weird as it did at first. I don't know if I was just getting used to it or if all the Christmas decorations made the place seem warmer and more cheerful.

"Merry Christmas!" Nurse Kelly said when she saw us. "Amber is giving all of you a Christmas present."

"What is it?" my mother asked.

"Amber is doing extremely well," Nurse Kelly went on. "She's definitely starting to gain weight—more than three ounces."

"Oh good," I said as we all practically jumped for joy.

"We've nicknamed her Chubby," the nurse said jokingly.

"Oh, I'm so happy," my mother said.

"Really," the nurse continued, "at the rate she's going, she'll be home before you know it."

"That's a wonderful Christmas present, isn't it?" my mother said, smiling.

"It's the best Christmas present of all!" I said.

My parents and I went through what had

become our regular routine of washing our hands and putting on gowns. I had a Christmas present for Amber—a brightly colored stuffed clown doll. I chose it because my mother explained that babies like bright colors.

When we got to her isolette, Amber was awake. I put the clown next to her in her little crib where she could see it.

Amber stared at it.

"Look," I said to my mother. "She likes it."

"She sure does," my mother agreed.

"Merry Christmas, Amber!" I said. "I love you."

We spent the whole morning and part of the afternoon with Amber. We were a family, even if we were spending our Christmas in the hospital.

Later that day our family was invited to Charity's house for Christmas dinner. We stopped off at home first and got dressed in our holiday best before heading over there. When we rang the bell, Zachary answered the door. He was dressed up in a plaid vest and a bow tie.

"My, don't you look festive?" my mother remarked when she saw him.

"I don't like this bow tie," Zach replied, tugging at his collar.

"Well, I think you look very nice," I said.

Charity's parents came to the door and welcomed us inside. Charity greeted me with a hug. She had on a beautiful dress that matched the plaid in Zach's vest.

"I love your dress," I said.

"My mom made it. We're all matching today—Mom, Molly, and I have matching dresses, and Dad and Zach have vests."

"How cute," my mother agreed. "Your mother is so creative."

I handed Charity a present.

"Merry Christmas," I said.

"Oh, thank you," she replied. "I have one for you, too." She went over to the tree, retrieved a package, and handed it to me.

"You open yours first," Charity insisted.

"What in the world is it?" I asked. I pulled away the colorful wrapping paper. Inside was a beautiful little wooden box.

"I found it for you in an antique shop," Charity explained. "I know how much you like that kind of stuff."

"Oh, Charity, it's gorgeous," I said, stroking the smooth, polished wood.

"Now open yours," I said.

Charity pulled away the paper and opened the tiny box.

"Oh, wow," she said. "It's a necklace."

"It's half a heart," I said. "It says, 'Best

Friends' and I have the other half." I held up the necklace that I was wearing.

"I love it, Brittany," she said, giving me a hug.

"You've really been a true friend," I said.

Just then Charity's mother called us to the table.

"Come on, everyone," she said. "Dinner's ready."

We all went into their dining room. The big table was brightly decorated with flowers and candles and gleaming china. A huge holiday turkey sat in the center, waiting to be carved. There were dishes and dishes of food—cranberries and stuffing, sweet potatoes and green beans, rolls, pumpkin pie, and a Christmas cake.

"Oh my," my mother remarked when she saw all the food. "It looks wonderful."

"Marvelous," my father agreed.

We were all seated around the table. Charity's father sat at the head of the table. Next were Mrs. McKay, Molly, Charity, and Zach at the other end of the table. I was seated across from Charity, and my parents were next to me. We all joined hands to say a blessing. Then everyone dug in!

Mr. McKay carved slices of turkey as Mrs. McKay passed the side dishes. Soon our plates were brimming with food.

My father raised his glass. "Merry Christmas to our friends," he said as we all clinked our glasses together.

I looked around the table. Everyone was so happy, smiling, filled with the holiday spirit. It was a real family Christmas. And even though Amber couldn't be with us yet, I knew she would be next year.

I smiled, raised my glass, and said "Merry Christmas, Amber!"

About the Author

As a child growing up in Florida, Deborah Abrahamson had an overly active imagination. "My mother told me that I kept the neighborhood kids captivated with my stories, even when I was very young," Deborah says. "By age seven, I was writing poetry, and at age nine, I made up my own newspaper."

Though she first became a commercial artist and illustrator, Deborah never lost the love of writing. "After I had children of my own, I rediscovered children's books and knew that that was what I wanted to write."

She currently lives in Seminole, Florida, with her husband, four sports-minded children, a rabbit, a spoiled cat, and a golden retriever. When not writing or taking care of the family, Deborah spends her time volunteering in the schools, as well as watching basketball, soccer, and little league games.

Ms. Abrahamson's first book in the Charity & Friends series is *Super Rich Switch*. This is her second.